Henrietta Hedge

written and illustrated by
Heather S Buchanan

edited by Nina Filipek
designed by Liz Auger

Copyright © 1995 Heather S Buchanan. All rights reserved.
Published in Great Britain by World International,
an imprint of Egmont Publishing Ltd., Egmont House, PO Box 111,
Great Ducie Street, Manchester M60 3BL.
Printed in Finland. ISBN 0 7498 2277 5

A catalogue record for this book is available from the British Library.

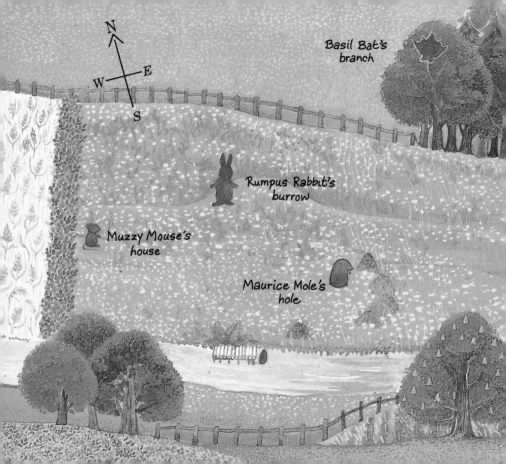

Basil Bat's branch

N
W E
S

Rumpus Rabbit's burrow

Muzzy Mouse's house

Maurice Mole's hole

Scampa Squirrel's
tree

Henrietta Hedgehog's
log

Buttercup Meadow
stretches from the Deep
Dark Wood in the north,
where Basil Bat and
Scampa Squirrel live, to the
small stream in the south,
where Maurice Mole has
his home.

Henrietta Hedgehog lives
in an old log on the east
side, and Muzzy Mouse's
straw house is under the
hedge to the west. In the
middle of the meadow
lives Rumpus Rabbit.

This is Henrietta's story...

H enrietta Hedgehog lived in a hollowed-out log at the edge of Buttercup Meadow. She knew all about the plants and herbs that grew in the countryside, and she made medicines for any animals who were feeling ill, and who came to her for help to get better.

B ut one day, it was Henrietta herself who was not feeling well. Two nights earlier, when she had been out to make a wish on the new moon, she'd forgotten to put on her scarf, and the evening was chilly. Now she was sneezing so loudly that Basil Bat could hear her as he flew past.

B asil went at once to tell Rumpus
Rabbit, Scampa Squirrel, Maurice
Mole and Muzzy Mouse. They were all
very sorry to hear that their friend had a
cold. "Poor Henrietta!" they said
sympathetically. "What could we do to help
her feel better?"

S tanding round Henrietta's bed, they offered helpful suggestions, almost falling over each other in their eagerness to be useful.

"She's too cold!" said Rumpus, piling on the blankets.

"No, she's too hot now," said Maurice, pulling them off again!

"She ought to have some medicine," said Scampa, finding a bottle that said 'For coughs and colds'.

Muzzy thought it would be nice if they spring-cleaned the bedroom to cheer Henrietta up. Soon the sweeping brush was out and the dust was flying. All the animals sneezed loudly as they rushed around, tidying the room.

"I can't stand much more of this," thought Henrietta to herself as she hid under the bedclothes.

T hen she had an idea. Sitting up brightly, she said, "I know what would *really* make me feel better. Some hot garlic soup. You could all go and find some wild garlic and cook some for supper. Take my big basket from beside the fire."

"That's a good idea," said all the animals enthusiastically. "Then we can stay here for the night, after supper, to keep you company." They set off for the Deep Dark Wood, where the best wild garlic grew.

The minute she was sure they had gone, Henrietta crept out of bed and wrote a little note. She just had to have some peace! If they were going to stay all night, she would never get to sleep. So she fled in the opposite direction across Buttercup Meadow to Rumpus Rabbit's empty burrow. Exhausted, she climbed into his string hammock, snuggled down under the cover, and slept at last.

The well-meaning animals arrived back at the log with their basketful of wild garlic. Muzzy got the frying pan out and the fire going. But Maurice found the little note by the bed. It said, "Enjoy the soup, and make yourselves at home. I've just gone away for some peace and quiet."

"Oh, dear," they sighed. "We've driven poor Henrietta away with our fussing and fretting. But we must find her and get her back into her bed."

So they set off in the dusk with lanterns. They searched the hedgerows and the woodland path, and they went on searching and calling for her all night long. But all the time, unbeknown to them, she was sleeping safely and warmly in Rumpus's burrow. When dawn came, they trekked back sadly to her house to make the soup for breakfast.

Luckily for Henrietta, the mole didn't like garlic soup so he went home to his hole to fetch some berry jam. He made his way back to the others by taking a short cut through an old tunnel which led out into Buttercup Meadow from Rumpus's burrow. The rabbit dug it himself once on an expedition to meet up with Mole underground, so it led directly back to Mole's little hole.

Henrietta, however, was in terrible trouble. When she first woke up in the dawn light she felt much better, and she had stopped sneezing. But when she tried to get up she couldn't. She was stuck fast, her prickles tangled up in the string of the hammock. The more she wriggled, the worse it got.

"Oh, I wish my friends were here now. I wish I hadn't run away and hidden from them," cried Henrietta.

I magine how surprised she was to see Maurice passing through the back of Rumpus's burrow, just at that moment, carrying berry jam. Imagine how surprised Maurice was to find Henrietta, completely stuck, swinging around helplessly in Rumpus's hammock!

In no time at all, Maurice had bitten his way through the netting and freed Henrietta, who rolled out and hugged him happily.

Then they walked back, paw in paw, to her log where soup was being served.

The animals were very relieved to welcome Henrietta safely home again!

"We've been so worried about you," they said, as they poured out a bowl of hot steaming soup for her.

She felt much better for drinking it and for seeing them all smiling at her. "I'm sorry, everyone," said Henrietta. "I realise now, you were all doing your best to help. And I am sorry about your hammock, Rumpus."

The animals sat story-telling round the fire all day, keeping warm and enjoying each other's company.

Henrietta curled up in her favourite chair, pleased that her cold had almost gone. She sent Rumpus home to fetch his hammock so that she could mend it by the fire that night, whilst he slept in her soft warm bed. Henrietta smiled thoughtfully as she sewed. "How lucky I am to have such good friends."

The End

TITLES IN THE BUTTERCUP MEADOW SERIES
BY HEATHER S BUCHANAN

RUMPUS RABBIT
HENRIETTA HEDGEHOG
MAURICE MOLE
SCAMPA SQUIRREL
BASIL BAT
MUZZY MOUSE